The Man Who Met the King

By

Gerard Goggins

Ambassador Books, Inc.
Worcester • Massachusetts

Library of Congress Cataloging-in-Publication Data

Goggins, Gerard E.
The man who met the king / by Gerard Goggins.
p. cm.
ISBN 1-929039-14-X (pbk.)
1. Spiritual life--Fiction. I. Title.

PS3557.O3235 M36 2002
813'.54--dc21

2002015517

Published in 2003 in the United States by Ambassador Books, Inc.
91 Prescott Street, Worcester, Massachusetts 01605
(800) 577-0909

For current information about all titles from Ambassador Books, Inc. visit our website at: www.ambassadorbooks.com.

Printed in Canada.

— In memory of Fred Harkins, S.J. —

The unexamined life is not worth living.

—Socrates, *The Apology (399 B.C.)*

Chapter One

The Pit

He was there every day, waiting for something.

I first noticed him a couple of weeks earlier. It was a beautiful Indian summer day, so warm and friendly, that for a moment I was able to escape from myself. There seemed to be a golden tinge around everything—the trees, the fading grass, even around the people. It was a scraggly looking park with scraggly people, but the sunlight and the shadows, the golden aura and the smells, made it seem lovely.

As I walked along, paying attention to my surroundings for perhaps the first time in weeks, I had a feeling that someone was paying attention to me. I glanced over at a bench where a man was sitting, but when I looked at him, his eyes were somewhere else. He was nondescript, in his late fifties or early sixties, maybe older or younger—I couldn't tell. There wasn't anything special about him. His clothes looked like normal, everyday clothes—not new, not old, just clothes.

And he was like his clothes. There was nothing distinctive about him. He wasn't ugly or attractive. In fact, I can't even remember exactly what he looked like. I'd know him if I saw him again, but if I was asked to describe him—tall or short? thin or heavy? clean shaven or a beard? color of eyes?—I just couldn't say.

Each day around noontime, I went through the park on my way to get a hamburger and fries for lunch. And each day, as soon as I entered the park, I would get the feeling that he was there and that he was observing me. He wasn't staring at me. I never even caught him looking at me, but I knew he was paying attention to me. And I knew that he knew that I knew.

He didn't make me uncomfortable. He didn't look like a person to fear. He made me curious. And that was a good thing. It got my mind off me for a minute or two.

My life had become a shadow. There was nothing to hold on to. It was all ambiguity. A kind of blackness gathered inside me like an infection, spreading through my mind and emotions, contaminating any sense of meaning or promise with despair. There was nothing in my life that I found pleasing. There was no joy or hope or even pleasure. Sometimes when I was able to sleep, I dreamt I was swaying in a light breeze, hanging from a branch with a rope knotted at my neck, and I felt at peace. Swaying gently, without consciousness—freed from my dark soul by the cool, soft wind.

I told no one. There was no one who I cared to tell and no one who cared to listen.

I wanted to get away, to take the trip that Hamlet talks about—the trip to the undiscovered country. And I knew that I was approaching the departure date.

And I think that the man on the bench knew it, too.

✧ ✦ ✧

Each day, as I went through the park, I felt him looking at me, and each day I walked closer to his bench and studied him out of the corner of my eye as I walked by. Sometimes he would glance up at me and make eye contact, but then his eyes would slowly sweep away. It was as if he was saying, "Yes, I notice you. But I'm not going to make an issue out of it."

He was completely unthreatening.

And so I got more and more bold. Each day I walked a little closer to him and stared at him a little longer. I don't know why I did it—perhaps to prove that I wasn't afraid.

Indian summer ended and the days got colder, not really frigid, but cold enough. The wind had an edge to it, and almost all the park benches were empty—except that one. He sat there every day, waiting for me, like he knew me and he was just waiting for me to say something.

So one dark, cloudy day, I stopped right in front of him.

He looked up at me, and this time his eyes didn't move away.

"I'm sorry you're so unhappy," he said.

"What?"

"I said, 'I'm sorry you're so unhappy.' "

I walked away without answering him. His words chewed at me. "What business is it of his?" I thought. "Where did he get his information? Who is he to say that kind of thing?"

The quicker I walked, the more angry I became. By the time I reached the other side of the park I was in a rage. I turned around and went back. I wanted to say something to him, something nasty, perhaps obscene. I was so angry I almost ran across the park.

But when I got to the bench it was empty.

The wind picked up, pushing a forlorn and dirty paper napkin across the sidewalk. It felt like it might start to rain any minute.

The anger drained from me. It was replaced by deep almost malignant melancholy, a sense of loss, of being bereft, abandoned and alone, and I wondered if I would ever see him again.

✧ ✦ ✧

I had a terrible night. I don't think I slept more than fifteen minutes. I was oppressed by the image of the man on the bench.

I spent half the night insulting him in imaginary diatribes, and half the night worrying that I had hurt his feelings and that I might never see him again.

It was demeaning, humiliating, absurd. I mean, I wondered why I even cared. My life was slowly sinking into the sewer, but because a man who I didn't know told me he was sorry that I'm unhappy, I became enraged.

What was he sorry for? Why should he be sorry for me? What did he know? Why did he even care?

I suppose what really bothered me was that he acted like he knew me, like he knew about the inside of me.

And there was another thing—the way he looked at me, as though he wanted to do something for me, as if I was broken and he wanted to repair me. Of course, that was impossible. He was so ordinary, so average. And yet I couldn't help noticing him. I noticed him all the time.

I never walked through the park without looking at him and wondering about him and wondering why he took notice of me.

He grated on me. He wasn't the kind of person you had to worry about. There was no sense that he wanted anything from me. He was just some nobody who thought a smile and a kind word could cure everything that's wrong with the world. I supposed he meant well, but I was sure he didn't know what life was really like.

I decided that I would no longer go through the park on my lunch hour. I would avoid him, and he would stop invading my consciousness.

But when it started to get light out, I began to look forward to lunchtime so I could go to the park and see if he was there.

✧ ✦ ✧

He was. And this time he was really paying attention. He kept his eyes on me as I walked toward him, and when I stopped in front of the bench, he looked right into me, not just into my eyes, but right into me.

I felt like crying. In fact I felt like crying so much that I couldn't speak.

"Would you like to sit down for a minute?" he asked.

I shook my head.

"I'm sorry you're so troubled," he said.

I thought, "Yesterday I was sad. Today I'm troubled. What will I be tomorrow?"

"Perhaps, you will be less sad, less troubled, and even happy," he said.

It was as if I had been slapped. He knew exactly what I was thinking.

"Are you a mind-reader?" I asked.

He didn't answer my question.

"Would you like to sit down?"

I sat down on the other edge of the bench, as far away from him as I could get.

"How do you know I'm sad?" I asked.

"I've dealt with a lot of people who are sad," he answered.

"Are you a shrink?"

"Not in the conventional sense," he said.

What did that mean?

"That means, I am not a psychiatrist, but I have the ability to help you."

This was eerie.

"But how do you know about me?"

"Perhaps we'll get to that later," he said. "Right now, the more important question is, do you want to sink into the sewer or do you want to have a life?"

I was speechless.

But he waited until I wasn't speechless anymore.

"I'm afraid of you," I said.

"There's no reason to be," he replied.

"Look, lunchtime is over. I've got to go," I said.

He didn't seem upset. He was very calm and understanding.

I got up and left him without saying another word and without answering his question.

Did I want to have a life? That was the question.

I took a few more steps and turned around to look at him.

He had already left.

And for the life of me, I still couldn't remember what he looked like.

✧ ✦ ✧

That night wasn't too bad. I was so tired that I slept soundly until about 5 A.M. And then, suddenly, I was wide awake. I immediately started thinking about the man on the bench. I tried to get him out of my mind but I couldn't. The weather was turning cold, and I was afraid he would stop going to the park. I was afraid that I would never see him again. I was afraid that I would not get a chance to answer his question.

My fear slowly drained out of me. I knew he would be there. He was not finished with me. And then the fear came back. I was afraid that he would be in the park, that I would see him again, and that I would have a chance to answer his question.

It was insane. There was a war going on inside of me. My mind went back and forth, back and forth, yes and no, no and yes, fear and hope. Yes, hope. Hope for what? I had no idea. I just thought that maybe there was a glimmer at the end of my tunnel, and I didn't know if I wanted the glimmer to get brighter or to get swallowed up in the darkness. It really was insane.

✧ ✦ ✧

He was still there, steadily watching me approach. He did not seem surprised. He just seemed patient.

"I am patient," he said. Was he reading my thoughts again? Or was it just a coincidence.

I thought I saw him smile, slightly.

"A coincidence?" I thought, and I tried to hold on to the words with my brain. I was sure he would say that there are no coincidences, but he just looked at me with that slight smile.

"Please sit down," he said.

I felt more relaxed. I sat more naturally, not hugging the far end of the bench.

After an awkward moment of silence, I decided to get it over.

"Part of me wants to have a life, and part of me wants to sink into the sewer," I said.

"Yes, I know," he said. "Part of you is your friend and part of you is your enemy."

I stared right at him, right into his eyes. They were filled with kindness.

He nodded and I thought he would say, "Yes, I am kind. I am patient, and I am kind."

But he just nodded as if he knew what I was thinking.

"Part of you loves you and wants you to have a life, to be happy, to be free, and to have meaning. And part of you hates you and wants to destroy you. That part of you is the worst kind of enemy. Not only does it want to see you destroyed, it wants you to destroy yourself," he said.

A chill wind blew across the park. Winter was at the threshold of the city, knocking to come in.

"How do you know all this?" I asked. "I mean, you may be right. But how do you know all this?"

Now the sky grew darker, and the wind grew stronger, stabbing the air with shrill whistling sounds. Dirt from the sidewalk swirled up and whipped across the park. It stung my cheeks and made my eyes water.

The smile left his face for a moment, and the wind was calm again.

"How do you know all this?" I asked again.

"That's not what's important right now," he said. "What's important is you."

I felt a sudden surge of joy. I'm not sure why. Was it because there was one person in the world who thought I was important? That I meant something? That I wasn't just another piece of rubbish bobbing up and down in the river of life?

The joy lasted only a second. I was leery of this man. I didn't know what he wanted or what I was getting into.

"I still have to know," I said. "I just can't . . . I've got to know. Do you understand?"

He nodded.

"Then I suppose I will have to tell you the story," he said.

"Good," I said. "What story? I mean, what do you mean, 'the story'? "

"It's a story about a man who met the king," he said. "But your lunchtime is over. We'll have to start tomorrow."

I knew just by looking at him that he wasn't going to answer any more questions. He had a sort of take-it-or-leave-it look on his face.

I shrugged. There was no law that said I had to come back the next day. I could take it or leave it then.

I started to walk quickly out of the park. I didn't turn around to see if he was still there because I knew he would be gone.

And then I had a very strange feeling, so strange that I felt the hair on the back of my neck tingle. I realized that the only reason this strange, nondescript man was coming to the park was to talk to me. He had this whole thing planned. He had set it up. He had set me up.

It was eerie. I decided right then and there that there was no way that I was going to listen to his story about someone who met the king of England or some other king.

I didn't know what this guy wanted, but whatever it was, he wasn't going to get it, because he wasn't ever going to see me again.

But I no sooner made the decision never to see him again than I knew that I would go back the next day. It didn't make any difference whether I wanted to. I knew that I would.

And I knew it was because of the pit—the black hole—that total darkness that was telling me to come home.

Chapter Two

Time Slows Down

The next day, I reversed my decision. I decided that I would not go to the park. But it didn't make any difference. There was a powerful force, a kind of magnetism pulling me there. Something in me decided that I would go to the park, even though I didn't want to go. I dreaded seeing this man again. I didn't know what he was going to say, but I was afraid to hear whatever it was. His words were like his eyes. His eyes looked right into me, and his words went right into me. They went right to the center of my being, and when they got there, they churned things up.

And he really hadn't said much yet. That's what was frightening. He seemed to be able to read my thoughts and to know things about me, maybe everything about me, especially the things I didn't want anybody to know.

It is very unnerving to meet someone who seems to know everything about you and who even seems to be able to read your thoughts. He has the potential to get inside you and open up every closed door and let out all the rot, all the thoughts and memories, the stench of life, the failures and stupidities, the lonely embarrassments, the rejections, all the fetid wounds that cripple me and that I hide from.

When I was a child, I had a dream that I was walking through a crowd of people who were staring at me because I didn't have any clothes on. There was no way to hide and no way to cover up. I just had to keep on walking. No one said anything. They just stared at me.

But that was nothing. The people in my dream couldn't see inside of me. They could only see my naked skin. They couldn't see the inner rot or smell the inner stench. They couldn't hear my thoughts or see my fantasies. But this man could. At least I thought he could.

The thought of someone seeing my fantasies, even the old fantasies, the ones I've forgotten, made me cringe. And it wasn't just the fantasies, it was all the stupid, petty, embarrassing thoughts I've had. I was afraid that this man had a video of my inner being, and that he could play it, and that I would have to watch it with him.

That was truly daunting.

✧ ✦ ✧

He wasn't there. The bench was empty. I stopped and slowly did a complete 360 degree turn. I looked at every corner of the park. He was not there. He hadn't shown up. All my worries and all my fears had been a waste of time.

For a brief second I was relieved. I could climb back into myself without being discovered. I could cover myself with the sad blanket of DARKNESS and turn away from everyone and everything.

But then I wondered why he hadn't come. Wasn't I important enough? Was I too boring? Did he dislike me? Had I offended him? Had he decided that I was not worth his attention? Or was it just that I did not mean anything to anybody?

When you're out in the country at night and you stand on the brink of the universe, it looks so vast and so cold and so impersonal. It is neither friendly nor unfriendly. It simply doesn't care. You might as well be nothing. You might as well let your pilot light go out.

One of the things I hate about being a human being is when I don't want something and then I'm disappointed when I don't get it.

I turned to leave the park and out of the corner of my eye I saw him sitting on the bench. He sat looking at me as if I was late and he had been there all along waiting for me.

"You have decided that you want to hear the story," he said.

I had forgotten all about the story, but I nodded anyway.

"Please sit down," he said.

A chill wind whistled through the empty trees. I hunched my shoulders and pulled my collar up. There was no one in the park except the two of us, and suddenly I felt that I was one too many.

"It's halfway through the lunch hour," I said. "Will there be enough time for the story?"

He smiled his little half smile. "Time is relative," he said.

✧ ✦ ✧

I'm not sure how to account for what happened next. It was as if I fell into a hypnotic state. As he began to speak, the sky cleared and the wind stopped.

The sun warmed the park and me, and my mood changed instantly. I felt very cozy and very comfortable sitting on the bench with this stranger.

Then something happened that was beyond my comprehension. It seemed quite natural, but in fact it was incredible. With his very first words the scene changed. As he began to speak I could visualize the characters, almost as if they were standing in front of me. His words seemed to create a kind of play, a drama which I could see and even hear.

I saw a little boy beaming as if he was filled with LIGHT. He was happy, almost ecstatic, and he seemed eager for life. His little hands stretched out as if he was trying to touch something—the future, perhaps, or joy or the essence of life itself. The child looked straight ahead, smiling at me, I think, or just smiling. And it was just as well that he did not look around, because behind him was DARKNESS. It was crowded and noisy, even chaotic, and it was slowly moving toward the little boy.

As I peered into the DARKNESS, I saw three faces. One was filled with RAGE and another with FEAR. I saw a third face, smaller, younger, which was filled with SADNESS. Gradually the SADNESS was replaced by FEAR, and then the FEAR was replaced by ANGER. As I watched, the ANGER turned to RAGE. The noise became louder and more chaotic, and the DARKNESS grew wider and higher and wider and higher, and came closer and closer to the little boy.

I looked at the man beside me on the bench. He just kept speaking, and I realized that I could not hear what he was saying, but I could see the reality that his words painted.

I don't think the little boy could see me any more than an actor in a movie can see someone in the audience. And I knew instinctively that I could not warn him about the DARKNESS that was moving toward him.

I turned to the man on the bench.

"They will hurt him," I said. "They will crush the joy right out of him. They will kill his spirit."

The man did not seem to hear what I said, or at least he paid no attention to it. He continued his word picture without acknowledging me.

At last the DARKNESS closed in on the boy. At first his radiance repelled it, but it kept circling him and enclosing him. Gradually, the LIGHT which shone from the little boy began to dim. It was being swallowed by the DARKNESS. He looked confused, and his little hands reached out toward the angry faces, but the faces became even angrier, and the child pulled his hands back. Now I could hardly see his face, but if I strained my eyes I could see it very faintly. It reflected the only bit of LIGHT in the DARKNESS. It was as if the child still had a little flame of light flickering inside of him—a pilot light that the DARKNESS and FEAR and ANGER and CHAOS had not extinguished.

And then the scene disappeared.

I turned to the man on the bench.

"I don't care for this story," I said.

He nodded. "Shall I go on? Or do you want the lunch hour to end?" he asked.

"There's more to the story?"

"Yes."

"Does it get worse?"

He looked at me with that little quarter smile of his.

"I want the lunch hour to end," I said. I looked at my watch. There were only five minutes left to the end of lunch hour.

Without saying another word, I hurried off. I knew I didn't have to say anything. And I knew he knew I didn't have to say anything.

And we both knew that I would be back.

There was something about that little boy that would draw me back.

Chapter Three

A Revelation

When someone slips over the edge from sanity to insanity, does the person know? Does he or she wake up one morning and say, "All right. It's happened. I've lost my grip. I'm no longer in reality. I have gone mad?" Or is insanity really believing that you have a grip on reality when you don't?

For half the night, thoughts like that skewered me. Was the lunch hour reality? It seemed like the story had gone on for a long time. Was time really relative? Could time slow down for me but stay at the same speed for others? Or is that crazy thinking? And if it is crazy thinking was this whole thing in the park crazy?

I lay in bed and stared up at the dark. "Is this whole thing crazy?" I whispered. "Am I crazy?"

And then I thought, "If I ask, I'm not. If I was really crazy, I wouldn't ask."

For the briefest second the image of the man on the bench floated in my mind.

It was a comforting image. It was a peaceful image. I knew that I trusted him, and I fell asleep.

But then I dreamt of the little boy. I saw his face smiling and his hands reaching out, and then I saw him swallowed into the DARKNESS. I heard the raging all about him, and I heard his silent sobs, the sobs that could not be uttered. And I saw the lightening flashes of his pain. I saw them piercing his body and tearing at his soul. And at the center of his being I saw the LIGHT growing dimmer and dimmer until it was almost out.

And then I felt the DARKNESS sucking me in. It had such force that it swept me right past the little boy into the deeper DARKNESS, and there I could make out the raging faces. I could feel their hatred and their venom. And as I looked into their glaring eyes I could see into their souls, and I saw that at the center of their beings there was only DARKNESS.

I woke up in a sweat as if I had a fever. And as I lay in the dark I could hear the raging voices of my dream. They told me that I really was crazy. They told me that I was a fool and that I was listening to a bigger fool. They told me that my life was utterly ridiculous and that my pilot light was out and that I was living on its fading afterglow but that I just didn't know it yet.

And in that dark night, I was filled with FEAR. I felt it charge through my body, tightening the skin on my temples and poisoning the pit of my stomach. I was friendless and alone, just like the little boy in the story and in my dream.

✧ ✦ ✧

At lunchtime there were no preliminaries. I went to the bench and sat down. The wind stopped, the sun shone warm, and my fear left me. I felt cozy and comfortable, and I knew that time was relative.

We sat for a moment without talking.

Then he turned and looked straight into me.

"How are you holding up?" he asked.

"As best I can," I answered.

He fixed his steady gaze on me and waited.

"I had a lousy night," I said.

He still gazed and still waited.

"I had a terrible dream, and then when I woke up, it was even worse."

"The enemy," he said.

I thought of my dream and its aftermath. As I lay in the dark I had trembled. More than trembled, I had literally shaken with fear. But there was no one in the room with me. There was no enemy there. It must have all been my imagination. It was the aftershock of a bad dream.

His gaze was steady, unmoving.

"What enemy?"

"The one who wants you bound in DARKNESS."

I didn't respond. I just sat there with my mouth shut.

He looked away and began to talk, and at once I could see the pictures his words were painting.

The little boy was older now, maybe six or seven. His face had none of the joy or anticipation that was there when I first saw him. Now it was like a mask. His expression was impassive with the slightest hint of dejection. The blackness and the screaming were everywhere. He could not escape it. I strained my eyes to see if his pilot light was still on, and as I did I realized that he was covered with welts and bruises as if he had been whipped and beaten. But the welts and bruises were inside him. They could not be seen by those around him, they could only be seen by looking at his soul, for it was his soul that had been subjected to such abuse.

I looked at the man on the bench beside me but he was gazing at the scene his words were painting. Like the boy in the scene he looked very sad.

I looked back at the word picture. The DARKNESS was growing deeper and more dense. The screaming was constant. The boy was surrounded by a black cloud of CHAOS.

I could no longer see his pilot light. But instinctively I knew it was still there despite the CHAOS and the DARKNESS. Somehow he was hiding the LIGHT so that the raging voices could not see it.

The voices in the DARKNESS seemed to know it was there too, or at least to suspect that it was there. They were confused. They thought the LIGHT was there but they could not see it. It could have been out. But there was something about the boy's face, perhaps a faint look of HOPE that told them they had not yet dominated him. Their rage was muted. They knew his LIGHT was not out, but they could not prove it.

The scene vanished and the man turned to me.

"Children are made to be loved, honored and affirmed, and they know that intuitively. That is why the most difficult thing to bear in life is utter rejection from those who should love us," he said.

My eyes were wet and there were tears on my cheeks.

"How long is this story?" I asked.

"Just long enough," he said.

"I'm afraid for that little boy. Will his pilot light go out?" I asked.

He eyes focused on mine. His face was utterly peaceful.

"That's up to you," he said.

Chapter Four

The Terror of the Night

I LAY IN BED WAITING FOR THE DARKNESS TO ATTACK ME.

I had no idea what the man meant. How could that boy's pilot light depend on me? How could I keep the DARKNESS from snuffing it out?

It was a story. It was the man's story. He was making it up or recounting it. I had nothing to do with it.

In my mind's eye I saw the boy's stricken face, and I saw the welts on his soul. Suppose his pilot light did go out. Whose fault was that? Not mine. I had not rejected him. I had not screamed at him. I was just watching his story. And every time I watched it, it got worse. And what I was really afraid of was that the story was happening now. It wasn't something out of the past; it was going on right now.

The boy's face looked so troubled. He was so helpless, so hopeless, so all alone. I wouldn't blame him if his pilot light went out. Suppose he let himself get sucked into the black hole. Why not?

"No! No! No!" a voice shouted. Was that me? Was I shouting? Had I been dreaming again?

I was soaked with sweat and trembling from the chill.

All the terrors of the night were in my room with me. I felt the HATRED that was aimed at that boy aimed at me. I felt the sneering and the scorn. I could sense their delight as they raged in the DARKNESS. They hated that boy and they hated me. And something told me that if I would join them in hating the boy, they would stop hating me. They would stop terrorizing me at night. They would leave me alone. They didn't care about me. They just cared about that boy.

As I stared up at the ceiling, I could see the boy looking straight at me as if he was waiting for me to do something—smile, perhaps, or join the others in screaming their hatred at him.

I was filled with FEAR, overwhelming FEAR, a tidal wave of FEAR. It engulfed me. It was drowning me.

"No!" I screamed. "No! No!"

The noise stopped. The room emptied of terror. Where had it gone? Where had they gone?

I stared up at the ceiling, and I saw the face of the man in the park. He was calm and peaceful.

"Go to sleep," he said.

And I fell asleep.

✧ ✦ ✧

I had questions. Who was the boy? Where was he from? Who were these people who hated him so? What did he have to do with me? What did I have to do with him? What was going on in my mind? In my dreams? In my room? Was this terror real? Was it just my imagination?

If this really was a story I was being shown, was it happening now or did it already happen? And how could I possibly be responsible for what happens to the boy's pilot light?

Who was the man telling the story? What did he have to do with the boy? Did he used to be the boy but now he was grown up? Was the boy his son?

And why did I feel threatened, as if I was in danger? It was as if I was locked into something I had no control over.

How did I get into this? And how could I get out of it?

✧ ✦ ✧

A very light snow was falling when I entered the park. He was already at the bench waiting for me.

"Maybe time is relative," I thought as I walked to the bench, "but I bet the weather isn't."

I brushed a light film of snow off the bench and sat down.

"Can you really read my mind?" I thought. He didn't answer.

"This is like waking up in the middle of a battlefield and not knowing who is fighting whom," I said aloud.

Instead of answering me, he gazed straight ahead. As he began to talk, the snow stopped falling and the sun broke through the clouds. I felt a tremendous peace. Maybe the weather is relative.

I knew that as soon as he started talking I would see another horrific scene, and yet I felt at peace, even though I knew what was coming.

✧ ✦ ✧

As he started talking, I saw what seemed to be thousands of people crowded together. They were all walking, but I had no idea where they were going. Somewhere among this mass of humanity, I saw him. He was older, now; perhaps twelve or thirteen, and the welts on his soul had been hidden. If you looked closely you could still see them, but if you didn't know they were there, you wouldn't notice them. I could see that his pilot light was still lit. In fact sometimes it would flare up and shine brightly and the pain would leave his face. But whenever it did, dark vapors would emerge from the crowd and surround him, the pain would return to his face, and his pilot light would dim. I watched that happen several times, and I noticed something else that seemed very strange to me. When the dark vapors came to surround him, a dark vapor emerged from within him and merged with the other dark vapors.

At first I could not tell where the dark vapors were coming from. But then I saw a group of angry voices in the crowd. They clung together feeding RAGE to each other. They kept watching the boy, pointing at him and screaming at him, but he either did not hear them or he had learned to ignore them. But every time the vapors emerged to surround him, they came from the group of angry voices.

I wanted to ask the man what the boy had done to make them so angry, and why that fact was missing from the story, but I knew I wouldn't.

✧ ✦ ✧

The scene changed. Now the boy was a few years older, almost a young man, of sixteen or seventeen, and for the first time his back was turned to me. He was wearing a large knapsack, and he seemed to be setting out on a long journey through a vast country.

But the path that ran before him was not an ordinary one. It looked like a huge game board. It wound through woods and hills and valleys, past lakes and precipices and dark caverns, and into a trackless desert that bordered an ominous forest. Some of the places seemed warm and friendly, with names like WISDOM'S ARMS, HOSPICE OF PEACE, and LOVING GLADE while others seemed cold or menacing with names like THE VALLEY OF DEPRESSION, THE ARTIFICIAL THICKET, THE HOUSE OF CONFUSION, and THE ARID ROAD. Far off in the distance, just before the road reached the horizon, there was a fork. One branch of the fork was illuminated by rays of sunlight but the other path was enveloped by DARKNESS.

The boy paused, as if waiting for a signal to start. He adjusted the knapsack and tugged at the shoulder straps as if its weight bothered him. As he did he turned to one side. I could not see his face, but there was something about the shape of his head and the way he stood that seemed familiar to me, and I wondered if I had met him before.

I looked at the man on the bench beside me, and the scene vanished.

"Do you understand what you're seeing?" the man asked me.

"I think so. At least I understand a little bit. I mean, maybe not. I'm not sure exactly what's going on in the story, and I'm not sure why you're showing it to me."

"This is the life story," the man said.

"I don't understand what you mean," I answered.

"Have you ever wondered what life is all about?" he asked.

"Yes, I have."

"Well, this is THE STORY OF LIFE," he said.

"The boy in the story—I have the feeling that I've seen him before," I said.

The man did not respond. He just looked at me with that quarter smile of his.

"Is the story out of the past or is it happening now?" I asked.

"Both," he said.

"Why is he carrying that knapsack? Is there food in it for his trip?"

"No."

"Clothing?"

"No. He doesn't need either for this trip. It's a spiritual journey," the man said.

"Then why is he carrying the knapsack?"

"It contains his past. He always takes it with him," the man said.

"You mean all the screaming and rejection and the welts on his soul?"

"Yes."

"That doesn't make any sense. Why would he take that stuff with him?"

"He can't help it. He doesn't even realize that he's doing it," the man said.

"But you said this is THE STORY OF LIFE—does that mean everybody does that?"

"Everybody carries the past with them. But not every past weighs the same," the man answered.

"You mean I carry my past with me, too?" I asked.

He smiled his quarter smile.

I looked away from him. "I don't do that," I said angrily. "I don't carry around a knapsack full of pain."

"You don't?"

"No," I said.

"Then why are you here?"

I was confused and I felt my anger building to the point of explosion. But when I looked back at him, my anger left me immediately.

"I'm not sure why I come here," I said.

He looked into me without saying a word.

"But I think you know something. I don't know what, but whatever it is, I have a feeling that it's important."

"Important for you or just important?" he asked.

"Maybe both," I said.

"You're almost ready," he said.

"Ready for what?" I asked.

"You're almost ready for tomorrow," he answered.

"What's going to happen tomorrow?"

"Lunchtime is over," he said.

I looked at my watch. He was right.

Chapter Five

Recognition

That night was brutal.

Something sinister menaced me in the dark room. I lay completely still trying to avoid thought, hoping for sleep, but Fear stabbed at me. It seeped into my body and assaulted my mind.

Was there something there? Was it external? Or was the menacing presence within me, and was I simply trapped inside my own thoughts—totally vulnerable, without any defense? I felt insanity calling me. I was certain that my mind was about to disintegrate.

I wrenched my body to the side of the bed and turned on the lamp. No one. Nothing. The room was empty, but I felt seething hatred and utter contempt directed at me as if an enemy was there, snarling and angry, lusting after the destruction of my spirit, scorning my fear, taunting my helplessness, and jabbing me with the implacable hand of HATRED. Indeed, there was a kind of joy in its hatred.

But was my enemy me? Or something outside of me? Was it all in my imagination, and was I really on the verge of madness? Or was it real?

I sank back on the pillow, and as I did, the lamp went out. I tried to turn it back on, but either the bulb burned out or there was a power outage.

The room was completely black. I could see nothing. But I could feel a tidal wave of evil engulfing me.

There seemed to be no escape. My destruction was at hand.

And then, from somewhere, a thought came to me.

"This is part of it."

The night, the dreams, the menacing DARKNESS, and the man in the park, the story, and the boy were all part of it.

And then I had another thought, in the form of a question.

"Do you want to go on or do you want to end it?"

My fear doubled and redoubled. I had heard about people who wanted to jump out of their skin, and it was a perfect description of how I felt.

Whatever was in the room with me was making it clear that I should not continue, that nothing good could come of it, but that something bad certainly would.

I sat straight up. The waves of FEAR still surged at me. But I felt another presence, and I thought of the man in the park.

"I want to go on," I said.

FEAR raged at me.

"I don't care about FEAR. I don't care if it crushes me. I want to go on," I said. "If I go mad, I go mad, but I will not surrender."

The HATRED and CONTEMPT drained from the room. I felt at peace. I knew intuitively that something of great significance was happening. It was life changing, or at least it had the potential to be.

And then FEAR was back. It told me that my situation was hopeless, that my destruction was inevitable.

"I want to go on," I said aloud.

But how could I go on. I was worthless—repulsive. The world would turn its back and close its ears to the sounds of my gnashing teeth. I was all, all alone. There was no one who could help me or would help me—no one who even wanted to help me.

"I want to go on," I repeated.

I felt a determination and a courage that I did not know I had. FEAR had done its worst, and it had not crushed me. HATRED and CONTEMPT had not destroyed me. I was not going to the country that Hamlet talks about. I was going to be.

I could feel the raging voices. I could feel their hatred. I could feel the welts on my soul. And I could feel that freedom lay ahead.

I lay back down. I knew that I was not alone.

"I want to go on," I said again and fell asleep.

✧ ✦ ✧

"The nights are part of this thing, aren't they?" I asked the man in the park as soon as I saw him.

"Yes," he said.

"Then the fear I have is part of it too," I said.

"Yes. FEAR is part of it, and so are TRUST and COURAGE and HOPE," he said.

"But I don't have to continue if I don't want to," I said.

"That's right. Whether you continue or not is up to you."

"It's very interesting," I said.

He did not respond.

"I want to go on," I said.

He nodded and began to speak in pictures again, and I saw the same scene as I had seen the day before. The boy had matured. He was now a young man and he was standing at the beginning of a winding path with a knapsack on his back. His back was still toward me, but I had the uncanny feeling that I knew him.

He turned around and looked at me, and suddenly I recognized him. I knew who he was. His face broke into a smile, and I was dumfounded.

The person in the story, the person with the heavy knapsack on his back, who was starting a trip, was me.

I looked at the man on the bench beside me.

He stopped speaking the pictures and returned my look.

"Do you still want to go on?" he asked.

"Absolutely," I replied.

As soon as I spoke the word, I became the person in the picture. I stood with the path before me, weighed down by the heavy knapsack of my past. I was the infant who had stretched out his hands for joy. I was the little boy who had been surrounded by dark vapors and who heard the raging voices. I was the boy with the welts on his soul. And now I was a young man. I was still not my age, but I was getting there.

The straps of the knapsack cut into my shoulders, and I knew that all I had gone through was in the knapsack and that I was carrying it around with me. I tried to slide the straps of the knapsack off my shoulders so that I could throw it away. But I could not move the straps. They felt attached to me, like they were glued to me or riveted to me, or that they were part of me.

I looked over my shoulder at the park bench, and I saw that I was sitting on the bench watching me. And I realized that I had been sitting on the bench watching me all along.

There was something else. The me on the bench was smiling as if he were my friend, a kind of older brother. Someone really cared about me. That felt good. It didn't matter that the person who cared about me was really me. Or maybe it did matter.

✧ ✦ ✧

I looked down the path, and I knew instinctively that I had already been to some of the places I was going to, and that I was still in the past catching up with my life. I didn't really care where I went as long as I got on with it. I wanted to go wherever I had to go in order to get to wherever it was that I wanted to be. The trouble was that I did not know where I wanted to be. I supposed that it would be a case of trial and error, and I quickly learned that I was right.

"Where do you want to go first?" a voice asked. I assumed it was the man in the park.

"To anyplace that is pain free," I answered.

"There are no places like that on this journey," the voice replied.

"In that case, I'll just start walking," I said.

I had not taken more than a couple of steps when I started down what was at first a gentle slope. As I went along I began to feel a tinge of sadness. The slope got steeper and as it did my sadness got deeper, and I began to feel the uselessness of life. Within a minute or two DEPRESSION enveloped me. It was like a warm, wet blanket wrapping itself around me, and in a way it was almost soothing. I wanted to stop walking. The trip was going to be too long and too difficult, and it would accomplish nothing. I wanted to lie down and not move. I wanted to give up.

I had wandered into a dismal place. The trees were bare and sickly looking. Weeds and brambles were everywhere. The path had become fainter and fainter until I could barely make it out. The skies above me were gray and brooding. One gaunt bird perched on a withered branch. It was the only sign of life that I could see. I sank to my knees, not wanting to go on but not quite ready to collapse.

And then I heard my own voice. It was coming from the park bench, and it was shouting, "Get up. Do not surrender. Get up."

And suddenly I was sitting on the bench looking at myself in the valley, and I could see that if I got off my knees and started walking I would be able to walk through this depression.

"Get up off your knees. Put one foot in front of the other," I shouted. "Don't argue. Just do it."

I started to do as I was told, but I had an overwhelming feeling that I could not do it. I was too weak. I was too tired. I was too sad. And what happened to me was of no consequence anyway.

"Get up," I shouted again. I looked at the man on the bench.

"Do you want help?"

I looked at the word picture and saw that I was still on my knees.

"Yes," I said. "Please help me."

He smiled at me, and suddenly I was back in the picture. I struggled to my feet, and I began to put one foot in front of the other. With every step I took I felt stronger and less sad. Finally, I knew I was certain that I could get out of this depression, and as soon as I realized that, I found that I was back on the path and free of SADNESS.

"Try to remember these lessons," the man on the bench said.

"How could I forget?" I asked.

"Most people do," he answered.

✧ ✦ ✧

It was exhilarating. I had been without HOPE and had survived. And now as I stood on the path and looked out toward the horizon, everything I saw was beautiful. Even though it was winter in the park, it was spring where I was standing. I could see the butterflies and hear the birds. I could hear the rushing water of a stream and feel the cool fresh breeze on my skin. Life was good. Here there was no pain. The man in the park was wrong. I was pain free. I was strong. I was not crippled by depression or the past. The knapsack was still heavy and the straps cut into my shoulders but I could bear the discomfort. It was not pain; it was merely discomfort. I could bear it. It meant nothing to me. If that was all there was to the past, there was simply nothing to be worried about. I was free, and I was ready for this adventure.

It is wonderful to feel your own strength, to know your power. I felt almost superhuman. Nothing and no one could stop me. I was Alexander and Attila and Cortez rolled into one. I had been liberated from that poor lonely creature with welts on his soul. I looked out at the world, and I was truly the master of all I surveyed.

I had the feeling that what happened to me was up to me—that I could recreate myself, and another sense of my own strength surged through me. I was filled with joy and confidence. I was a new me.

I looked down the path and saw that a hundred yards ahead of me there was a small path which branched off to the left. I had the sense that down that path there was someone waiting to see me—a young woman—I think. No. I am sure it was a young woman. Somehow I could see her face. There was something mysterious about her demeanor as if she held an important secret. She was attractive without being showy. She seemed quite serious, and yet, I thought I detected something joyful about her.

I started walking toward the small path. It was narrow and stony and it was lined with brambles and thorn bushes. It was obvious that not very many people used the narrow path, and it was easy to see why. It was a very difficult way to walk. Still, I thought of the young woman, and I was ready to start down the path when I noticed that there was another path branching off to the right. This path was much wider and well trodden. It was lined with pretty bushes, and it was very inviting. From down the path I could hear music and laughter. I decided that the young woman with the attractive face could wait. I wanted to see where this path went. Even as I did so, I felt a pang as if I was making a bad choice, but I was so intent on seeing what was ahead of me, I ignored my instinct which said I should stop and return to the narrow path.

The way curved into a dense thicket. Great trees arched above me so that I could not see the sky. As I walked along, it got darker and darker. Not much light could penetrate the thick foliage. Then after a few steps the path widened and I was suddenly in a kind of room in the forest. It was bright and loud. I looked up and I still could not see the sky. The light that filled the area was artificial. All around me there were people chatting and dancing and laughing. They were all sharply dressed and they seemed almost to glitter like jewelry. The women were very stylish, but they wore thick makeup, the way some of the women who work at cosmetics counters wear makeup. They were all dressed seductively—revealing necklines and dresses with slits up the thighs. I knew that I had merely to approach any one of them to be entertained.

My breathing quickened and my pulse beat more rapidly. I felt like a lion surveying the field. A hand rested on my arm and I turned to see who was touching me. It was a very beautiful woman with silky black hair and a perfect smile. She seemed to emit a kind of aura which surrounded me and pulled me toward her. She looked into my eyes with a kind of hunger I had never seen before.

I had a fleeting thought of the young woman waiting down the difficult path, but the beautiful woman with the silky black hair tugged my arm.

She was very tempting.

I could feel my heart beating as I stepped closer to her. She looked straight at me, and I returned her look, but as I did I could see into her inner being, and I could see the DARKNESS inside her which hid the welts on her soul. I realized that she was looking for something that had nothing to do with me. As a person, I did not matter to her, and she could not matter to me.

I pulled my arm away. She looked surprised, questioning me with her eyes. I shook my head, and her surprise was replaced by indifference. She drifted into the crowd.

Another hand touched my arm. I turned and found a young man with the same hunger in his eyes. And I saw his DARKNESS and I knew he had welts on his soul. I pulled my arm away and he was gone.

I moved through the crowd. Eyes stared at me. Hands reached out to me. They all looked the same. Men, women, it made no difference. They were hungry and they wanted me to satisfy their appetites.

"Don't go," a voice said. "Please. You don't understand. We are free. You are free. Experience the pleasure, the absolute pleasure. You are in a place where there are no boundaries. There are no commitments, no responsibilities. Everything is allowed. Why not enjoy it."

I shuddered.

"You don't belong here," another voice said. "You're not up to it."

I turned and saw a much older man. At first I thought he looked refined and sophisticated, and then I saw that it was a façade. Just below his surface there was a brutal nature. He was a man who delighted in demeaning others. He looked at me with a contempt that bordered on hatred. Being in his presence reminded me of the terror-filled room with the seething HATRED.

"How many lives have you crushed?" I asked, and I was surprised by my boldness.

"Not nearly enough," he said.

"You will not crush mine," I said.

"The game is not over," he replied.

"Where's the path out of here?"

I realized that the exit was behind him.

He folded his arms and stood smugly in my way.

"You can't get out of here," he said.

My knapsack suddenly felt terribly heavy. It dug into my shoulders. I wanted to sit down and rest. But I thought of the me on the bench and I knew that I had to go on.

"Get out of my way," I said.

He bristled, and seemed even more determined to keep me from leaving.

I stared into his eyes, but I could see nothing. I looked harder trying to see his darkness, trying to see what made him what he was. But I could see nothing inside of him.

He seemed startled by my look, and after a moment, he stepped aside.

I was surprised, and I looked at him even more intensely.

He turned and walked away.

I saw the exit. There was a sign hanging over it which said: YOU ARE NOW LEAVING THE ARTIFICIAL THICKET WHERE NO ONE IS REAL. I did not see the sign as I was coming in, it can only be seen on the way out. If you never leave THE ARTIFICIAL THICKET, you never learn the truth about it.

✧ ✦ ✧

The air was exhilarating. I felt as if I had been freed from a dungeon. It took a moment for my eyes to adjust to the sunlight, but when they did, I saw the narrow path, and I could visualize the face of the young woman who was waiting. It was so different from the faces I had just come from. Instead of being filled with DARKNESS, it was filled with LIGHT. I wanted to meet her, to talk with her. But the path looked difficult. It was almost overgrown with thorns and brambles.

I hesitated. Perhaps I should stay on the main path, I thought. It was wider and easier.

But the image of her face would not leave my mind. When I first saw her image, I thought she was plain, perhaps somewhat attractive. But as I studied her face in my mind's eye, she seemed very beautiful. I wondered if I would ever see her again, and if I ever did see her again, I wondered if she would even speak with me.

✧ ✦ ✧

I turned to the man on the bench. "That young woman . . ." I left the unfinished sentence hanging in the air.

"Yes?" he said looking squarely into my eyes.

"She seems very . . ." I hesitated but his look was gentle. I knew he would not sneer at me or demean me. "She looks very beautiful," I said.

"She is very beautiful. But most people don't notice her beauty."

"Do you know her?"

"Yes."

"Do you know her name?" I asked.

"Her name is WISDOM," he replied.

"That's a funny name," I said.

He smiled.

"Is she my HEART'S DESIRE?" I asked. I really didn't know what I was saying. I didn't even know that I had a HEART'S DESIRE.

"No."

I must have looked crestfallen.

He smiled again. "She is not your HEART'S DESIRE. But you will never find your HEART'S DESIRE without her," he said.

✧ ✦ ✧

I studied the narrow path and again WISDOM's face came to mind. She looked so beautiful that I hoped the man on the bench was wrong. I hoped she was my HEART'S DESIRE. And then I had a kind of vision. I saw the figure of another woman off in the distance. She was dressed all in white, and I felt my heart drawn to her. I tried to see her face but I knew that in order to do that I would have to get much closer to her.

✧ ✦ ✧

As I sat on the bench looking at me and wondering what I was going to do next, I noticed that I had grown older. I was taller now and stronger. I had reached my mid-twenties.

I turned to the man on the bench. "Can I rest for awhile? I'm tired," I said.

"Lunchtime is over," he answered.

Chapter Six

In Pursuit of Wisdom

I didn't know if I was dreaming or if I was awake or if it made any difference.

"You are making a bad choice," a voice said from behind me. I recognized the voice. It was the brutal man I had met in The Artificial Thicket.

I tried to turn around, but my body felt as if it was paralyzed.

I made believe I didn't hear him.

"You are young and inexperienced. You are inexperienced aren't you?"

I didn't answer.

"You know nothing of power, the joy of ruling, of having others do your will. You have no idea what wealth can do for you or how people will worship the ground you walk on. You own nothing except that heavy knapsack that you carry around. And you don't even know how to use it. You don't know how much power you can draw from it. You can use that knapsack so that your hatred strengthens you. You can avenge yourself on those who hated you. They will either bow to you or be destroyed. And your power will attract those you want to attract. Not the floozies with the slit dresses and the painted faces. You will attract real women, beautiful women, cultured women who love power, who seek it out, who adore it."

I didn't answer.

"You can choose a life devoted to seeking WISDOM, but WISDOM is a joke. WISDOM will do nothing for you except to rob you of enjoyment and keep you from your destiny."

I didn't answer.

"If when you go back into the vision, you will turn around and come back into the dark thicket, I will change your life. I will make you forget your knapsack. I will give you so much pleasure you will never want to leave the thicket."

"You are a liar," I said.

"What?" His voice was threatening.

Suddenly he was right in front of me. His stare went straight through me, but when I looked into his eyes, there was nothing there.

He was unnerving. There was something very nasty about him. I wanted to get out of there, to get away from him, but I stood my ground. And still I did not know if this was a dream or whether it was really happening.

"What did you say?" His tone was vitriolic.

"I said that you are a liar." My eyes were fixed on his. I did not waiver. "You lied to me in the vision, and you are lying to me now," I said.

He smiled as if amused, but even his smile was nasty.

"This is the truth. You are weak and you are a coward. You think the man on the bench will help you, but he won't. You are just another experiment for him, and when he sees that you can't stay the course and you just want to quit, he'll drop you just like he dropped all the others. Then you will turn to me and beg to be my friend, and I will remember what you called me. No one loves you. No one cares for you. You are something of a freak, a cast off, a quitter. Do you remember how you cried? And how you never stopped crying inside?"

Images of the past flooded my mind.

Suddenly he was gone and the dream or whatever it was ended, and the morning sun streaked through the window. But I could still see his leering, smirking, sinister face.

✧ ✦ ✧

My life was out of control—it took place in the park and in the dark of night. I was in the vision and out of it. In one way I was only a witness to what was happening to me, as if I was in a rudderless boat being pulled along by the current. In another way I felt that in some mysterious fashion I was steering the boat, that I could bring it to the shore at any time and get out. One minute what was happening to me seemed impossibly absurd, and the next minute, I felt that my eternal fate would be determined by what I was going through.

Who was the man in the park? And how did he know me? Who was the brutal man? And what difference did I make to him? Why would he bother to invade my dreams? And he had invaded them. He had not popped out of my subconscious. He was an entity. What difference did I make to him? Or for that matter, what difference did I make to the man on the park bench?

I knew that I could ask the man in the park all of my questions and that he would listen politely and smile, but he would not answer them.

"Be patient. When you are ready for the answers to your questions you will have them without even asking," the man in the park said as soon as I saw him.

Somehow I knew that he was right. And I had known that all along. Not knowing the answers to my questions was part of the journey.

But I still had questions and the most pressing was—if the attractive woman named WISDOM who disappeared down the narrow path was not my HEART'S DESIRE, was it the woman I saw dressed all in white?

I sat on the bench and I was back in the vision.

I looked down the narrow path. It was almost completely overgrown. My shoulders ached from the weight of the knapsack's straps, and a cold wind blew in my face. I could not bypass WISDOM and have my HEART'S DESIRE. The wind blew with greater force and sleet slashed at my cheeks. I looked back at the park but the sleet was so thick that I could hardly see myself sitting on the bench.

Perhaps the brutal man was right. Perhaps I was a coward, and all this was an experiment that would fail. The path looked hard and almost impenetrable. If I started down it, I could get lost and never escape from the vision. Even if I didn't get lost, I might never find WISDOM. It all seemed so difficult and hopeless. I thought of turning around and going into THE ARTIFICIAL THICKET to find the brutal man. And then I saw his sneer again, and I decided I would rather get lost and freeze to death going after WISDOM, than to have anything to do with him.

I knew that if I did not go after WISDOM, I might as well be dead. My life would have no meaning. The welts on my soul would never be healed, and I would never find my HEART'S DESIRE, whatever it was. And so I took the first step in my pursuit of WISDOM. It seemed completely foolish to go down the narrow overgrown path in seeking the vision of someone I had never met. But I did it anyway. Step after cold step, bramble after bramble, thorn after thorn, with slashing sleet, and aching shoulders, I went down a winding path, stumbling, tripping, falling, aching, struggling to continue, with part of me telling me I was stupid to continue, and part of me singing for joy that I had spurned THE ARTIFICIAL THICKET, and had risked everything to find someone I had never heard of before.

And suddenly WISDOM came to me, and for the first time I saw her as she was: radiant, gentle and kind, and eager to help me. She took my hand and drew me towards her, and we walked into a sun-filled glade where there was no wind and no sleet. I could not take my eyes off her. At first she seemed quite plain, but the longer I looked at her the more aware I became of a subtle beauty. It was not something that one could see at first, but I knew that the longer I knew her, the more beautiful she would become, like an ageless flower unfolding.

"Take off your knapsack and sit down," she said.

I was about to tell her that I could not get the knapsack off when I slid out of the straps and it fell to the ground.

"Do you know why you carry that around with you?"

"No," I answered.

"Because you have never looked at what's in it," she said.

"I don't have to. I know what's in there. I lived it. It's my past."

"It's more than that," she said. "It's a big part of your present."

"How can it be?"

"It weighs you down. It keeps you from your HEART'S DESIRE," WISDOM said.

"I don't even know what my HEART'S DESIRE is," I said. "Is it that other woman I saw?"

WISDOM smiled. "She is part of your HEART'S DESIRE."

"Who is she? What's her name?"

"She is LOVE."

"Can I meet her?"

"Not as long as you have to carry that heavy knapsack around," WISDOM said.

"That's crazy," I said.

"No," WISDOM answered, "that's life. As long as you refuse to look at what's in the knapsack you cannot know WISDOM and you cannot know LOVE."

"I don't believe you," I said.

WISDOM looked at me sternly. "It's not that you don't believe me, it's that you don't want to believe me. You are afraid to look at your past. So the past is keeping you from knowing the truth about yourself and about others. You are letting FEAR rule your life. As long as you do that you will never be happy or free, and you will certainly never really love anyone."

I remembered what the brutal man had said. I even heard his voice. "You are weak and you are a coward."

I knew I would have to look in the knapsack.

I undid the buckles and threw back the flap.

"I'll be right over there. I'll be available if you want help," WISDOM said.

Inside the knapsack, there were a number of metal boxes. Each of them was padlocked.

"Stick around," I said.

I started to take the boxes out of the knapsack. Each box had a word inscribed on it. The first was SORROW, then came ANGER, and then FEAR, and then HATRED. There were a couple of others that I did not look at too closely. "How do I get these boxes open?" I asked.

"There is one last box in the knapsack," WISDOM said.

I reached down as far as I could and felt the top of the box. I pulled it out and put it next to the others. It was inscribed MEMORY.

"MEMORY is the key to unlock the other boxes," WISDOM said.

"How did they get locked?" I asked.

"You locked them," WISDOM said.

I picked up MEMORY. It was the only box without a padlock. "How do I open this one?" I asked.

"Just lift the cover," WISDOM said.

I hesitated.

From behind me came the sound of someone snickering. It was a nasty, demeaning laugh. I looked around but I saw only WISDOM.

"COURAGE," WISDOM said.

There was another snicker. This time it was almost a snarl. I knew it was the brutal man, even though I could not see him.

I opened the box, and as I did everything changed.

✧ ✦ ✧

I found myself in a large dark hallway. There were doors to the left and to the right. Each of them was closed.

I was about to call out to WISDOM to ask her where I was, but I realized instinctively that I was the house and I was inside me. My house was a house of darkness and closed doors. It was a house of suppressed sounds coming from behind the doors—sobbing, screaming, shrill laughter, taunting, teasing. It was a house of chaos and pain and confusion.

"I'll go through this place room by room," I thought. As I wondered where to begin, the sobbing grew louder and I followed the sounds to a door marked SORROW. They grew louder still—heart rending, pitiable.

I opened the door and stepped inside. The room was even darker than the hall. In one corner, I could barely make out a young boy, sobbing short choking sobs, huddled listlessly against the wall.

As my eyes adjusted to the light, I could see that his eyes were swollen from the tears.

"What's the matter? Why are you crying?" I asked.

"I'm alone and unloved. No one cares about me. No one will help me. I've been abandoned," he sobbed.

"Perhaps I can help you," I said.

"You can't help me. Not you. You can't help anyone."

"How do you know that?" I asked.

"You are so stupid," the boy said. "Don't you understand who I am? I'm you."

"But you're only five or six," I said. "You can't be me. I'm an adult."

"If you're an adult, then I'm what an adult looks like," the boy said. He sobbed as he spoke.

"Come on, lets get out of here," I said.

He stopped sobbing. “I’m not moving,” the boy said.

“I’ve carried you around all my life. I’ll carry you out of this room if I have to,” I said.

He looked surprised.

“Let’s go,” I said.

“All right, I just want to get my list.” He bent over and picked up a stack of about twenty pages.

“What’s on the list?” I asked.

“I have written down every bad thing that was ever done to me, said to me, or said about me,” he said.

“So I’ve been carrying that around too,” I said. “Come on. Let’s go to the next room.”

The boy smiled a vengeful smile, and held out his hand. I took it and led him out of SORROW and brought him to ANGER.

“Should I knock?” I asked.

“Don’t be stupid. Just open the door.”

I was so surprised by the rudeness of the answer that I hesitated.

“You are such a jerk,” the boy said through clenched teeth. “Open the door.”

I did as he commanded. The walls of the room were painted black, and red bulbs glared from the ceiling.

The boy dropped my hand and bolted into the room.

“Get in here,” he screamed. “I’ve been waiting for this

forever. I've been waiting to tell you what I think of you."

"I thought you were SORROW, but now you're ANGER," I said.

"SORROW fuels my ANGER and ANGER turns my SORROW to HATRED," the boy said.

"Against me?"

The boy was enraged. "Of course against you. Do you see this?" He waved the stack of papers in front of my face. "Do you see all the things that you let happen to me, all the things you did nothing about?"

I remembered the dark vapors attacking him as a child. I remembered the raging and the screaming, the hatred and rejection, and as I remembered it, I felt the pain.

"I did all I could," I said.

"All you could? All you could?" the boy screamed. "Just what was that?"

"Look into me," I said. He looked away.

"Look into me now," I commanded.

Very reluctantly he looked into me.

"What do you see?" I asked.

"I see a pilot light," he said in a dejected tone.

"I kept the pilot light lit," I said. "That was the best I could do. And now I've come back to redress the wrongs and to help you grow up."

He already looked a couple of years older. "Can you do that?" he asked.

"I think so. Come on. Let's get out of here," I said.

This time he didn't resist. He didn't take my hand either. He seemed a little too old for that.

✧ ✦ ✧

The sounds of CHAOS had subsided in the hallway. There was no sobbing or screaming, and yet I felt a tension that perhaps I had not noticed before because of all the noise.

We came to a door marked HATRED.

"We've already experienced that. Let's keep moving," my companion said.

"Maybe this is different. Can you feel the tension?" I asked.

The tension increased and it had a magnetic affect on me. I felt that on the other side of the door, there was a tidal wave ready to surge at me, and yet I felt compelled to open the door, almost as if I had no choice. But before I could touch the handle, the door slowly opened as if by its own accord.

I looked around but WISDOM was no where to be found, and so I stepped inside the room marked HATRED.

My mood changed instantly. Everywhere I looked I saw things I loathed—old people, young people, stupid people, fat people, skinny people, women, men, different people, all people. They were weak and whining, strong and arrogant, sly and silent. None of them could measure up, and I saw my hatred reflected in their eyes.

And I felt sick—viciousness storming through me, strangling my soul, suffocating my hope, burying my HEART'S DESIRE. In my desperation I thought of WISDOM, and as I did she stood beside me.

"You are not ready for this room," WISDOM said. "You have to go to the SECRET room first."

"What SECRET room?" I asked. "That wasn't one of the boxes in my knapsack."

"Yes it was. But you piled all the other boxes on top of it so that it wouldn't be noticed."

"You mean I hid it from you?" I asked.

"You hid it from yourself," she answered.

By this time we were back in the hall.

"I still don't see the room marked SECRET," I said.

"You have to go through FEAR to get there," WISDOM said.

She guided me through a door and into a room that was hardly bigger than an upright coffin. I was filled with panic. I wanted to turn around and run, but WISDOM held me fast. We were standing in front of a door I had not noticed before, although I don't see how I could have missed it. It had a large padlock and a sign that said: "SECRET ROOM—NO ADMITTANCE—CONTENTS EXTREMELY DANGEROUS. COULD CAUSE DEATH OR PERMANENT PSYCHOLOGICAL INJURY."

"No wonder I hid the box," I said. "I don't want to go in there."

WISDOM smiled at me.

"What's the matter with you? Stop smiling! Don't you see I'm in mortal danger?"

"Do not let FEAR paralyze you. It is not real. It is a smoke screen that obscures reality."

"You mean I have to go in there," I said.

WISDOM still smiled.

I summoned up my last ounce of courage and I reached out to touch the padlock, and immediately it fell away, and the door slowly opened. I stepped into the room and I saw that on my left there was a man in a purple cloak sitting on a throne. He was wearing a beautiful crown inset with large diamonds and other precious stones. He was very regal, very proud, and all-together quite striking. I didn't recognize him at first even though he looked very familiar. I was so mesmerized by him that I forgot about WISDOM. I was about to bow down before him, when I suddenly realized who he was. The man on the throne was me.

"I am so handsome," I said aloud. "I'm a king, a ruler. That's me. What a wonderful discovery. That's really me. That's who I am. Somehow I knew it all along. I could feel it. I'm a king."

I looked at WISDOM expecting her to be overjoyed, but her face was somber, almost stern.

"That's a reflection in the mirror of your own ego," she said, pointing to my right.

I turned and saw the real throne and the real king looking at himself in the mirror. There was a throne, but it was made of cardboard boxes. Sitting on it was a three-year-old with a soiled diaper. He had a paper crown painted with yellow paint sitting atop his head. I looked back at the mirror of my ego, and he looked regal and handsome, like a real king.

"I am so handsome," the three-year-old shrieked. "I'm a king, a ruler."

He glared out at me. "Have WISDOM bow down to me and do my bidding," he said.

I turned to WISDOM. "Have I been carrying this around all my life?"

She smiled.

"Every three-year-old wants to rule the world," she said.

"But I'm not a three-year-old."

I looked back at the child on the throne, and shook my head. It was true. The words I had uttered a few minutes before rang in my years. "That's me. What a wonderful discovery. That's really me. That's who I am. Somehow I knew it all along. I could feel it. I'm a king."

"You look pretty silly," I said to the three-year-old. "It's time to abdicate." He closed his eyes, covered his ears, stamped his feet and started to shriek.

"It's no good," I said. "The truth is you're not a king. You will never be a king. You're just a little brat with a dirty diaper. Throw away that silly crown and get off the throne."

I took the crown off and threw it on the floor, and immediately I started to grow. I stepped down from the throne, smiled, and disappeared inside of me.

"TRUTH is an extremely powerful tool," she said. "Now that you know how to use it, you're ready for that other room," WISDOM said.

"Before we go there, I'd like to ask you something," I said. "You know about the man on the bench."

WISDOM smiled.

"In my first vision, I saw an infant who was full of joy and anticipation. He, or should I say 'I,' was reaching out toward the future and toward life. I seemed so happy with such a wonderful potential, how did that infant turn into the little brat with the dirty diaper sitting on a make-believe throne?"

"You were filled with LOVE and GOODNESS. And those around you were filled with ENVY and ANGER. Their message to you was that you were worthless and unlovable. The more you tried to prove them wrong, the more they attacked you. Finally, in order to prove your value you began to fantasize, and in your fantasies you became more powerful and more beautiful than them or anyone else. But at the same time, part of you believed they were right, and you tried to erase your own feelings of being worthless and unlovable through your fantasies. You created your own kingdom and became your own king," she said.

I didn't know what to say. I knew she was right. I had failed terribly.

"You didn't fail," she said. "Your past is part of your future."

"Then my future is lousy too," I said.

"Only if you walk around with a cardboard crown and a dirty diaper," she said.

I heard myself laugh. It was a most unfamiliar sound.

We left the SECRET room the way we had come in, but FEAR was gone. As we walked toward HATRED we passed the doors marked SORROW and ANGER. Both of the doors were wide open, and both rooms were bright and clean and quiet.

"ANGER doesn't last when the infant king is not in control," WISDOM said.

✧ ✦ ✧

HATRED was another thing altogether. It was not loud, but there was an unpleasant undercurrent, a tension that was so taut it made a discordant noise. As soon as I entered the room, I wanted to leave, but WISDOM compelled me to stay.

"Look around," she said. "Do you see the different kinds of hating here?"

There were several groups clustered throughout the room, but I couldn't tell one from another.

"They all look pretty much the same," I said.

"That's because they're all related," WISDOM replied. "But if you look closely, you can see the differences. See, the group on the left?" She pointed to a rather drab, listless group. "They are the haters who know you and direct their envy and their anger and their frustration at you in the form of hatred."

"These are the people in the vision who released the dark vapors?" I asked.

"Yes. And over there are the people who hate because they have been harmed. They are the revenge seekers."

The haters she pointed to looked wounded and very angry. Their eyes were red with blood and their faces were pointed like knives.

Beyond them was another group. They were very frightening. They looked almost like rabid dogs ready to leap at the throats of the weak.

"These are the people who hate for a cause," WISDOM said. "They hate because they believe their god tells them too, or they hate because it makes them feel superior, or they hate because it gives them a kind of joy. It is their hatred that gives them energy. They have no mercy and they seek none."

There was one other group, way at the back of the room. They looked very distinguished and very calm. They looked as if HATRED was the furthest thing from their minds.

"They are the exploiters," WISDOM said. "They are the people who gain by the poverty of others. They are the people who do not understand that CONTEMPT is HATRED without the passion. It is a cold dissociation from most of humanity."

"And they are all in me?" I cried. "That can't be. I'm not like that."

"They are all in everyone to a greater or lesser extent," WISDOM said. "In some they are hardly noticeable. In others they dominate the personality."

"What makes them that way?" I asked.

"They are ruled by their infant kings. In one he is a whiner. In another he is a tyrant. In another he is utterly hateful. In another he is selfish to the point of complete contempt for others."

"But my king has been dethroned. He's no longer a king."

"He's a king in exile," WISDOM said, "and he longs to return to power."

My heart sank.

WISDOM smiled. "He cannot return to power unless you allow him to, and that will only happen if you join the haters."

I looked over at the people who hated me. "What about them? They're not really inside of me. They really hated me. They hurt me. What do I do about them?"

"They are indeed inside of you," WISDOM said. "And they will stay there as long as you resent them."

Suddenly I felt my resentment, and I could feel the infant in me reaching for it like a king reaches for a scepter.

"How do I stop resenting them?" I asked.

"Look at them," WISDOM said. "Look into their souls."

I did, and I saw their welts, and I saw the door to the SECRET room that was locked deep inside of them.

I saw their anguish, and I looked for their pilot lights but I could not find them, and suddenly I felt like weeping.

"Yes," WISDOM said, "they are the prisoners of their inner tyrants."

"Will they ever escape?" I asked.

"We'll see," WISDOM said.

As I watched, the people who hated me seemed to fade away.

"What about those others? Should I look into their souls?" I asked.

"There is more to them than their inner tyrants," WISDOM said. "They are under the influence of an outside force."

At that moment, I looked into a far corner, and I saw the brutal man leaning against the wall staring at me.

"He's my enemy," I said. "What's he doing in here?"

"He shows up everywhere. He is the catalyst that sets off HATRED. He is the seducer of the inner tyrants, the power behind their thrones," WISDOM said.

"But what is he doing inside of me?"

"Biding his time," WISDOM said. "He is hoping that your infant king will get back in power."

"Can he do that? Can he take over again? The knapsack is off. I'm dealing with the past," I was starting to panic.

"There is only one way to keep the knapsack off," WISDOM said.

"Tell me."

"LOVE. If you want to be free, LOVE. It is the antidote to HATRED and ANGER, CONTEMPT and SELFISHNESS," WISDOM said.

My panic grew. "I don't know anything about LOVE. I don't know what it is. I don't know how to do it. I don't even know if it exists."

WISDOM touched my shoulder. "You know more about LOVE than you think. The seed of LOVE is within you. And when you find LOVE, the seed will blossom, and you will be transformed. HATRED will flee. It cannot coexist with LOVE."

"You mean I will meet someone who will love me, and her love will transform me?" I asked.

"No," WISDOM replied. "When you love, truly love, without selfishness, without conditions, without trying to use LOVE as a currency to get what you want from others, then by the very action of loving, you will be transformed."

"Is that possible?" I asked.

"There is only one way you can find out," WISDOM said. "You must find LOVE. Find her and let her fill the rooms that have been emptied by MEMORY and by TRUTH. Then you will know why you are on this journey."

I sighed. I thought the journey had ended. Now it seemed it was really just beginning.

"How will I know LOVE when I find her? What does she look like?" I asked.

"She looks like me," WISDOM said. "She's my identical twin."

"Is she far away?" I asked.

"The journey from WISDOM to LOVE is not a long one, but it can be very challenging," WISDOM said.

The man on the bench stopped speaking and the vision vanished. He turned to me.

"You should rest for a while. Think about WISDOM. Think about what she has taught you. It will be nourishment to help you through your journey," he said.

"Is finding LOVE that tough?" I asked.

He didn't answer.

I began to hope we could put the next leg of the journey off for a day. "Is lunchtime over?" I asked.

"We have plenty of time," he answered.

Chapter Seven

In Search of Love

I have learned that if you would seek Love, you must first go through the desert. But as I stood wearing my knapsack, ready to set out on what I hoped would be the last leg of my journey, I thought that finding Love would be almost effortless.

My knapsack did not seem very heavy now. In fact, I hardly noticed it, probably, in part, because I was so excited. I knew that Love is wonderful. In fact, that was all I knew about it, except that people fall in love. I thought it must be like falling into a pile of pillows and that the most difficult part of the process would be relaxing so that I could just gently fall into the wonder of Love. Then whoever I fell in love with would make me happy.

As I walked down the path my steps grew bolder and my strides grew longer. I felt like singing. Just a little while ago, I don't know if it was days or hours, LOVE seemed impossible as if it had no application in my life. And now I was on the path to find LOVE. I wanted to sing I was so full of expectation. I would meet my HEART'S DESIRE and she would think I was wonderful—as if, as if—I stopped there because I did not want to finish the thought, but the thought went through my mind anyway. She would think I was wonderful as if I were a king.

I don't know where WISDOM was at that moment, but I really did not want her to throw cold water on my imagination. After all, I thought, look what I've been through. Look at all the pain I've endured. Look at how brave I was to face up to ANGER and HATRED. I had COURAGE. I had ENDURANCE. I was strong. Of course, she would think I was wonderful. If she didn't, that would mean she didn't love me. If she didn't think I was, or at least I was like, a king, she wouldn't be worthy of me.

I was so deep in thought, I almost missed the sign. In fact, if I didn't have to duck to get under it, I would have missed the sign: TURN HERE FOR THE GIRL OF YOUR DREAMS.

This was so easy. After all I had been through; at last everything was falling in place. There were even road signs to point me in the right direction. This was much easier than going down the narrow path to find WISDOM—who didn't seem to be around now anyway.

As I turned off the path I immediately saw a wide door that swung open before me. I stepped into a beautiful room that was decorated with drapes and mirrors. I saw a red velvet chair which looked very comfortable, and I instinctively knew I was supposed to sit in it. As I did, I saw that on the far wall there was another door. It was marked: EMPLOYEES ONLY—DO NOT ENTER.

The lights dimmed and very soft, very romantic music began to play.

I heard a voice ask, "Are you ready?"

I didn't answer because I didn't know who was being asked the question. I thought that maybe THE GIRL OF MY DREAMS was being asked if she was ready.

"Are you ready?" the voice asked again. It sounded a little familiar but I could not place it.

"If you're asking me, then the answer is yes," I said.

At that moment, the most beautiful woman I had ever seen stepped through the door.

I couldn't believe it. An incredibly beautiful woman was walking directly towards me, and what is more, she was looking at me as if I really were a king.

She walked right up to me.

"Hello," she said. "Do you like what you see?"

"Absolutely," I answered.

She turned and looked at her reflection in one of the many mirrors on the wall.

"I do too," she said.

She turned back to face me.

"Do you like my eyes?"

I nodded.

"And my lips?"

"Yes," I said.

"And my figure?"

"Of course," I almost shouted.

She turned and looked in the mirror again. "I do too," she said.

I was puzzled.

"What about me?" I asked.

"What about you?" she replied.

"Do you like what you see?" I asked.

"What you look like is not important," she said. "What you have is what is important."

"What do you mean?" I asked.

"You don't have to be handsome," she said. "I have enough beauty for both of us. If people see us together, they'll know that you are special or I wouldn't be with you."

My excitement started to fade.

"So what do I have to have?" I asked.

"The normal things—money, status, power."

It would have been easy to lie and say I had lots of everything, but it seemed much better to simply tell the truth.

"I don't have those things," I said.

"Then I'm not THE GIRL OF YOUR DREAMS," she said, and turned and walked back through the door.

I was about to get up and leave when the voice said, "Next."

The woman came back out through the door and walked up to me.

"Hi," she said.

"Wait a minute. We just finished talking," I said.

"That wasn't me. That was NARCISSISTIC. She's just totally self-centered. It's a good thing she rejected you," the woman said.

"You look exactly like her," I said.

"I look like her but I'm not her. All the girls of your dreams look exactly alike," she said. "But we're not exactly the same. I don't spend all day looking in the mirror. I don't care whether you have money or status or power. I'm not like that at all. I'm interested in you, not what you have."

"Really?"

"Of course. You look so strong and so masculine. I bet you are strong. Are you strong?"

"Strong enough I guess."

"Do you think you could pick me up and carry me?" she asked.

She did not look heavy at all.

"Sure," I said.

She smiled. "Oh, good," she said and bent down and hugged me. I hugged her back.

"Stand up and show me," she said.

I stood up and slipped my left arm under her shoulders and my right under her knees and lifted her up.

"Oh, you are strong," she said. "Can you carry me out of here?"

"Sure."

"And do you think you can carry me on THE ROAD OF LIFE?"

"I guess so. Sure," I said.

"Then I'm really THE GIRL OF YOUR DREAMS?"

"You must be."

"Then wait right here. I just have to get my bag and then we'll start on THE ROAD OF LIFE," she said.

She ran back through the door and returned a moment later dragging a heavy suitcase.

"Come on," she said. "Pick me up and let's go."

I picked her up.

"Don't forget my bag," she said.

I reached down and grabbed the suitcase. I could barely get it off the floor.

"What's in there?" I asked.

"I don't know," she said. "But I've carried it with me all my life," she said.

I set her and the suitcase down. “That’s your past. You’ve got to open that up and look inside. You’ve got to lighten the load. I can’t carry that thing and you.”

“But you’ve got to. I need your support. I can’t get through life carrying that thing around by myself. And I can’t just throw it away. That’s me. That’s my life. That’s everything I have.”

“If you will just look inside, it will get much lighter. I know. I’ve done it.”

“But you’re strong,” she said.

“Not strong enough to carry somebody else’s load,” I answered.

Before she could respond, the voice said, “Next.” She left the room, and a moment later she was back.

“I’m not them. I am not NARCISSISTIC and I am not DEPENDENT. I am not self-centered, and I certainly don’t need anybody to carry my load. I’m perfectly capable of taking care of myself,” she said.

She studied my face briefly. “In fact, just by looking at you, I’ve fallen in love with you. You are the perfect man for me. You are handsome, you are strong. I can tell you have incredible potential. I just love you. No, more than that, I adore you.”

“You do?”

“Of course I do. And when you see what I can do for you, you’ll adore me, too.”

"What can you do for me?" I asked.

"Everything," she said. "You need someone like me. You have all this potential and so far you have done absolutely nothing with your life. And do you know why? Because you haven't had anybody to show you how to live and how to get ahead. You need someone—me—to plan for you and to guide you. You need someone who will show you how to dress and make sure you eat right, someone who pushes you to get the right job and to get ahead. I can map out a success story for you that you won't believe. Behind every great man, there's a great woman. And I'm a great woman who can make you a great man. I can transform you."

I stood up. "Your name must be CONTROLLING," I said.

"Yes. How did you know?"

"I'm leaving," I said.

"Without me? You can't I'm THE GIRL OF YOUR DREAMS," she said.

"You may be THE GIRL OF MY DREAMS, but you are certainly not my HEART'S DESIRE. And I see that there is a real difference between the two," I said.

✧ ✦ ✧

I was back on the path, but now my strides were less confident. It seemed that every time I was sure of myself,

I ran into trouble. Now, I was wary of a misstep which might cause me to trip, so my pace was slower.

As I walked along, I began to feel the weight of my knapsack. It was not as heavy as it used to be, but its straps were irritating my shoulders and irritating me. The scenery gradually changed. The green grass and tall trees gave way to shrubs and brown grass, and then the shrubs and brown grass gave way to a few parched weeds and finally to a wasteland. As I looked around, I saw sandy tracts. Nothing was growing anywhere.

The sun grew warmer and I grew thirsty. Part of me wanted to turn around and go back, but something inside of me kept pushing me forward. I don't know how long I walked or how many dunes I crossed, but it seemed like I was walking for a very long time. I grew more tired and irritable to the point of being angry. The longer I walked the more the straps dug into my shoulders and the more irritable I became.

"Stop for a moment and rest," a voice said.

I turned and looked and saw a fair young woman smiling at me.

"Where did you come from?" I asked.

She did not answer.

"What do you want?" I asked sharply.

The young woman seemed startled by the harshness of my tone.

"I came to see if I could help you," she said in a quiet voice.

"How can you help me? You can't carry my knapsack. You don't have any water. How can you possibly help me?" I said in a voice that was almost a snarl.

She looked very sad.

"Who are you, anyway?"

She did not answer. Instead she turned and walked away. In a moment she was gone, and I knew that LOVE had fled me.

I became even more angry. She should have known that I was so concerned about myself that I couldn't recognize her. She should have introduced herself. She knew I was looking for her. And if she really was LOVE, I thought, why didn't she bring me a glass of water?

I walked on, not paying attention to where I was going, and as I walked, I felt the inner king trying to take over. I stopped and sat down. The sun was hotter than ever, and I was dryer than ever. I felt like a wilted weed. And I felt like a fool. LOVE had come to meet me and I had snarled at her.

"O, LOVE," I cried aloud, "will you give me a second chance?"

And there she was. Out of nowhere, she was sitting directly in front of me and smiling. "She must really want to help me," I thought.

"I'm sorry I snarled at you," I said.

She continued to smile at me, but I hardly noticed her smile, and I completely ignored the cool brightness that surrounded her. She was appealing beyond words, but it was very hot and I was in the desert. She looked so comfortable that it was annoying.

"You said that you wanted to help me," I said.

"Yes," she agreed still smiling.

"Do you think you could take my knapsack and carry it for me for a while?"

LOVE looked surprised.

"Nobody can carry your knapsack but you," she said.

"Then how can you help me?"

"I can fill your heart," she said.

"With what?"

"With me," she said.

"I would rather have water," I said sourly.

And for the second time, LOVE fled me.

And in the desert heat, tired, hot and very irritable, I remembered the words of WISDOM: "LOVE. If you want to be free, LOVE. It is the antidote to HATRED and ANGER, CONTEMPT and SELFISHNESS."

I struggled to my feet. I had offended LOVE, I did not think that she would return. I took a few steps forward, and now the weight of my knapsack caused the straps to dig deeply into my shoulders. It was very painful. I wanted to stop, but something impelled me forward, and there she was again, waiting for me. The smile had returned to her face.

"You came back," I said.

"Yes."

She was radiant in a way I had never seen before. She was luminescent as if a LIGHT within her was filtering through her being and giving her an aura. She was, I thought, beautiful.

"You are very beautiful," I said.

She smiled gently.

"In fact, you are almost perfect," I said.

She continued to smile.

"And indeed you could be perfect, if you would . . ."

Her smile was replaced with a look of sadness, and with a sigh she said, "You are not ready to meet LOVE."

I could not argue with her. I knew she was right. She had come to me three times, and three times I had allowed self to reject her.

And so, for the third time, LOVE fled from me. I felt in my heart she would never return.

✧ ✦ ✧

A fierce wind came up and whipped sand across the dunes, stinging my face. I had to lie down and bury my head in my arms to keep the sand from getting in my eyes and nose.

"You have failed LOVE," a voice said. "But it is not much of a failure. LOVE is a mirage. She does not really exist, and even if she did, who could measure up to her. She's too sensitive. She's incapable of taking constructive criticism. She's too good for you. She's too good for anybody. Have you ever met anyone who was filled with LOVE? Of course you haven't. It doesn't happen. It's a fairy tale."

"But just because you have failed at love, you're life is not over. You still have THE GIRL OF YOUR DREAMS. She hasn't gone anywhere. Don't tell me she's NARCISSISTIC or DEPENDENT or CONTROLLING. Everybody is. But not everybody is beautiful. THE GIRL OF YOUR DREAMS is sensational. Anybody in their right mind would choose her over LOVE. With the GIRL OF YOUR DREAMS you have something to show off and something to work with. The trouble with LOVE is she's independent and she has such a high standard. Theoretically that's okay, but in practice it just doesn't work. You can control THE GIRL OF YOUR DREAMS. It might take some time, but there are techniques which are available. You can let her know you have a temper. You can sulk and be unresponsive. You can belittle her until she will do anything just to shut you up. And then you will have a raving beauty that will be like a puppet. You pull the strings and she dances."

The wind had stopped. I picked my head up and looked around to see who was talking. It was the brutal man who always turned up at my worst moments.

"I can call her, and she'll be here in an eye blink."

"I have seen LOVE and I have seen THE GIRL OF MY DREAMS. And you're right. There is no comparison. And in my immaturity and stupidity, when I was feeling bad for myself, I rejected LOVE, not once but three times. But having seen LOVE, I know there is no substitute. Maybe I will never find her again, and maybe I will. But I know I will never be truly happy without her. And I would certainly not be happy if I accepted a self-centered, controlling, dependent substitute," I said.

"You really are stupid," he said.

"I have heard enough from you," I answered. "Get out of here."

✧ ✦ ✧

It was dusk by the time all of this had transpired. The hot winds had turned cold, and I was sweating and shivering at the same time. I felt sick and defeated. I had no energy and no desire to move. I curled up to get warm, and I lay without moving and without thinking.

Voices in the desert shouted that I was a fool, and the voices echoed so that I heard them again and again.

"You will never be loved," the voices shouted. "You are unlovable. You see how LOVE has fled from you, not once, but three times. You will live alone and you will die alone. Your life will amount to nothing. Do you remember the black hole? Do you remember your desire to take the journey Hamlet talks about? It is time now. It is time for you to go to that undiscovered country. It is time for you to disappear into the eternal night. Only then will you escape being a fool. As long as you exist you will never be happy."

I felt too weak to argue. Perhaps they were right. Perhaps I would never be loved. They were certainly right that I was a fool. But they were wrong about the black hole and the undiscovered country. And weak as I was, I still knew that I had the strength to persevere. I wasn't going into the black hole. This was my ROAD OF LIFE and I would travel it until it ended.

I am not sure if what happened next really happened or if I was hallucinating because of my fever. But I saw the brutal man standing a few yards away from me. He was dressed as an usher in a theater, and he held one end of a red rope in his hand. The other end was attached to a brass pole. The rope held back a long line of people who seemed to be waiting to be admitted to an important event.

"One at a time, please," he said. "One at a time."

He let the rope drop for a moment and admitted the first person in line. It was an elderly man with a severe face who walked over to me.

I pulled myself into a sitting position and looked up at him.

"I was told that you can help me," the man said. "But I doubt if you will want to speak with me, because you're probably so much better than I am. After all, I have spent my entire life without ever loving."

"Well, I'll help you if I can, but I have to tell you that I'm no better than you are," I said. "I met LOVE three times and was so nasty to her that she fled three times."

The man's face contorted with rage. "How do you think you can help me? You're no better than a fool. You're a thousand times worse than me. No wonder you're in this desert. I hope you never get out of it. I hope you die here," he shrieked. He reached down and slapped me across the face, and spun around and walked away.

"Next please," the brutal man said.

A conservatively dressed woman in a business suit and sensible shoes walked over to me. "I was told to come and ask you for help, but if you don't want to speak to me, I'll understand. After all I'm poor. I have almost nothing. Who would want to speak with me?"

"I'll be happy to speak with you and help you in any way I can. If I had money, I would give it to you. But I own nothing. I have nothing to eat and nothing to drink."

She swung her pocketbook and hit me across the bridge of the nose.

"How dare you speak to me! I don't converse with bums. Don't you so much as look at me again," she said and stormed off.

"Next please."

A young man with empty eyes and a bored expression was next to approach me.

"Will you talk with me? I'm so stupid that nobody wants to talk with me. But the man over there said you'd be happy to talk to me."

"You can't be any more stupid than I am. I rejected my HEART'S DESIRE."

He kicked me in the chest. "You are really dumb," he said, and then he kicked me again before he walked away.

I looked over at the line. It was very, very long.

"Next please," the man said.

I struggled to my feet. "Hold it," I said.

I walked over and stood next to the brutal man and looked at the long line of people.

"Each one of you has come here to look down on me. You think that if you find out that I am poorer or more stupid or just worse off than you, it will make you feel better. You think that by slapping me or kicking me, it will give you a kind of status. But it won't help you at all. Instead of becoming better, you will become worse because you have tried to solve your own problem by hurting another human being. It just doesn't work."

The brutal man dropped the rope. "All together," he announced.

And they all ran at me, kicking and punching and screaming and spitting.

When I woke up, night had come. The desert was very cold. The sky was filled with stars, but the sky was cold too. My entire body was sore. My face was cut, and my clothes were ripped. It felt like I had been hallucinating, but perhaps I hadn't been. I thought of all the people who had attacked me. They had been manipulated by their inner king and by their pasts and by the brutal man. They were slaves, imprisoned by their hatred and their anger. I was sorry that I had not been able to help them.

I got to my feet and began to walk. My knapsack, which had been so heavy, was now surprisingly light. But my bruises made walking difficult.

"Come over here," I heard a woman say.

It was too dark to see who was speaking. I started to walk toward the sound of her voice, and as I did, I heard the engaging sounds of a rushing stream.

"Sit down," the woman said.

I did as I was told.

"You aren't THE GIRL OF MY DREAMS are you?" I asked.

"No," she replied. "Did you want THE GIRL OF YOUR DREAMS?"

"No. I just wanted to make sure you weren't her."

"I see that you have been injured," she said. "Let me make you comfortable."

She removed her coat and bundled it into a pillow.

"Lie back," she said.

"But you'll freeze without your coat," I said.

"No I won't. I'll be fine."

She gently pressed her hands against my shoulders and I sank back until my head rested on the pillow she had made with her coat.

Without further conversation, she lit a fire to keep us warm, and then she gave me a cup of water to drink and some bread to eat. When I was no longer thirsty and hungry she washed my wounds, and before she had finished I fell asleep.

✧ ✦ ✧

In my dream there were two flowers. One was crimson and one was blue. They were planted about a foot apart, but I could see that they wanted to be closer together. So they did not grow straight up. As they got taller they leaned toward each other, growing closer and closer until finally they were touching. As time passed, their stems wound around each other until it almost seemed that there was only one flower and that it had both crimson and blue leaves. The more they grew together, the more beautiful they each became. And soon new buds sprouted from them until they looked more like a beautiful shrub than two separate flowers.

When I awoke, she was still there, sitting opposite me, staring into my eyes, but I could not see her face because it was veiled in shadows.

"Thank you for your kindness," I said. "Thank you for everything you've done, for the water and the bread, for cleaning and bandaging my wounds, and for the fire."

"Do you know who I am?" she asked.

"I can't see your face," I answered.

"But do you know who I am even though you can't see my face?"

"You are LOVE," I said.

"That's right," she said, and moved closer to me so that I could see her face. She looked just like WISDOM.

"We're inseparable," she said.

"You fled from me three times, and you still came back."

"Of course, LOVE is constant. I did not leave you because you were unkind; I left you because you were not ready for me. I knew that you needed to go through the desert, but I planned to come back to you."

"But I treated you so badly," I said. "I really was a fool. I don't understand why you came back."

"I saw the seed of your goodness," she said.

"Then you've seen something that I haven't, something I don't even know about."

"You've seen it. You call it your pilot light. But it's the seed of your goodness, and it was planted in you by the king."

"The king? What king?"

She smiled indulgently.

"But the seed was being choked by the weeds of life, and it was in danger of dying. I suppose you would say that your pilot light was in danger of going out. But during your journey, the weeds have been pulled out one by one. And now your seed is turning into a plant, and I think that when it is full grown, it will be quite beautiful."

"Even so, what good will that be? You've seen me in action. You've seen how self-centered and controlling I am. LOVE runs away from me."

She laughed.

"Goodness can't help but love. The more your goodness grows, the more you will love."

She must have sensed my doubt.

"Be still and I will show you a vision," she said.

I obeyed her, and soon I saw a young woman standing before me. She looked very much like WISDOM and LOVE. At first she appeared merely attractive, but as I looked into her eyes, I was able to see her soul, and I was overwhelmed by her beauty. Her soul was like the sun, bright and warm, with a powerful gravitational force that drew me towards it, and I knew that my heart was filled with LOVE.

The vision ended, but I sat silent and still for a long time, feeling as I had never felt before.

"Who is she?" I asked.

"She is your HEART'S DESIRE," LOVE said.

"But where has she gone? Will I ever see her again?"

"Do you remember your dream?" LOVE asked.

"The two flowers?"

LOVE nodded. "You have a mutual destiny," she said.

And with that she vanished from my sight, and I was alone by the fire. A moment later I found myself sitting on the park bench.

"The story has come to an end, hasn't it?" I said to the man on the bench.

"Yes and no," he answered. "You have caught up with your past and stepped into the present. But there is a future."

"My HEART'S DESIRE?"

"Yes."

"But is that it? Is it like a fairy tale. I find my HEART'S DESIRE and that's the end of the story?"

"Not at all," he said. "Have you looked at your pilot light lately?"

I looked into my soul. "It's blazing," I said.

"Then I have a job for you," the man said. "I want you to rekindle the pilot lights of others."

"What others?"

"Those who are filled with DARKNESS and FEAR and HATRED and ANGER; those whose spirits are suffocating, whose lives are without meaning, those who want to go into the black hole and the undiscovered country."

"There's millions, maybe billions of people like that," I said.

"You are not the only one with a blazing pilot light," he answered. "Do what you can, and that will be enough."

"And what about my HEART'S DESIRE?" I asked. "How will I find her?"

"You have a mutual destiny. Remember your dream of the two flowers. You will enter each others' lives at the right time," he said.

"I have a feeling that now that the story is over, you won't be here tomorrow," I said.

"You've come a long way," he said. "This is my last visit to the park."

"Final question," I said. "You told me the story was about the man who met the king."

"Yes," he said.

"Are you the king?" I asked.

He smiled.

"Or are you a man who met the king?"

He smiled.

"Or am I . . . ?" My question trailed off into silence.

His earlier words came back to me: "Be patient. When you are ready for the answers to your questions you will have them without even asking."

I looked away, and saw THE ROAD OF LIFE. It had changed. In the distance there was no longer a fork in the road, with one way leading to DARKNESS and the other to LIGHT. Now the road ran straight and disappeared into the LIGHT.

When I looked back, the man was no longer there. In his place, there was a profound silence, filled with the knowledge of goodness and love and the presence of majestic power. I was at peace. For a long time after he left, I sat and reveled in a sense of beauty, in the vision of my HEART'S DESIRE, and in the warm, bright glow of my pilot light.

I had no idea what lay down the road but I knew that the story was not over.

About the Author:

Gerard Goggins is a former newspaperman and an avid classical scholar. His reporting has ranged from presidential politics to the ballet. His novel *Half-Wits*, has been used as a text in courses on morality in a number of colleges and universities. In 1994, he received the national Catholic Press Association award for best newspaper column. He is also the author of the critically acclaimed novel, *The Anonymous Disciple*. He and his wife, Deanna, live in Central Massachusetts.